THE CHAPTER

A Short Story

by

Don Kasparoza

KASPAROZA BOOKS

New York

Also by Don Kasparoza

For Blood And Loyalty

A Novel

www.ForBloodAndLoyalty.com

ISBN: 978-1502363923

www.TheChapter.tv

Facebook.com/TheChapterTV

Proudly dedicated to

Mario Diaz, Rafael Ramirez,

and

The Epsilon Executioners

In addition to every pledge who ever left our house crying.

Thank You for Your Support.

THE CHAPTER

THE BEGINNING

In basements all across Upstate New York, their names rang out. And down below in their own basement in Upstate New York, on the walls, some of their names were spelled out. But, it wasn't just the Brothers that scared them. Some pledges, the macho kind, could have cared less about the rumors. Many came from bad neighborhoods. Fatherless homes, troubled families. Most had been through much worse than what a bunch of college kids could throw at them.

But then there was The House.

That old, *mysterious*, gigantic 3-story house all the way down the long dead end on Vine Street was the kind of place that made a pledge's knees buckle. Their stomachs hollow. Some would even say that it made ghosts look for someplace else to haunt. It made them turn around. This house was taken.

But also, different: 47 Vine was unlike all the other houses in that desolate, rust belt of a neighborhood. It was older. It was painted a solid dark blue, and was built, and shaped unlike its peers. In fact, 47 Vine had been around since just before The Depression. Since Prohibition. Almost 31 years before the others even existed. Making it the only one that looked, and felt like, a fortress.

And that's how they treated it.

Its occupants were soldiers.

They were a cadre.

Because while the house might have been old, a confirmed fire hazard, to a bunch of kids who came from nothing it was without a doubt their castle, and underneath its massive three stories, three humongous floors with 20 large bedrooms that made it resemble a ghetto mansion off a ghetto MTV *Cribs* more than anything else lied the basement. It got cold down there. There were no electric space heaters in the winter. Sometimes, there was even asbestos. But right now, outside, there was snow on the ground.

But, down in the dark, very dark basement, as the six pledges looked around... all they saw was death. *Delta Death*, it was written on the concrete wall in front of them. The unfinished basement was nothing but concrete and graffiti. With random objects everywhere, across the walls read random mementos like *Alpha Amputations*, *Beta Bombs*, *Gamma Guts You*—even *Tau Tortures*. It was a kidnapper's dream.

As well as any pledgemaster's.

Every time another Kappa Chapter came down here to destroy some skutches they left their mark. And in front of these pledges, the founder of this Chapter, a hulking, 6'4", 30 year old Puerto Rican alpha male with shoulders like a Mack truck left his mark with his balls.

Don Victor, as the pledges were to refer to him, in his full Marine Corps fatigues pissed on the wet floor in front of them. Letting them know where they stood in life.

They tried not to think about it. All six of them, standing there at attention, side by side in size order in a tight line tried not think about the obvious things like how they'd been starved, lost at least 30 pounds each and looked like they'd caught cancer during the Holocaust. However, it was hard. They were surrounded.

All around the room a small army of 20 Brothers dressed in dark blue Kappa baseball jerseys with gold lettering on them stood in silence. Leaving them in fear. Especially the one Brother standing across from them holding a fire hose. It dripped dirty water.

The pledges weren't just shivering, they were soaked. What used to be their proud dark blue uniforms had been ripped to shreds. Even a bum wouldn't want them. Covered in dirt, sweating out grime, at this point just trying to survive they looked like they'd been through hell. In fact, they felt like prisoners of a war.

Exactly what Don Victor had hoped for.

Freezing, weak and outnumbered, with their heads shaved and two of them sporting fresh cases of ringworm the boss of this room gave them an update:

"Let me tell you something, you skutch-ass niggas. That you already know. This is not just any Chapter. This is The Valence University Chapter. The Chapter Among Chapters. The Chapter Among Chapters in The Latino Fraternity Among Latino Fraternities. But, if you want to be a part of this? If you stupid motherfuckers want to be Kappa men? Then first, you got to be regular men. And, do you know why?"

Don Victor singled out Number 6.

In fact, he always singled out Number 6, the tallest, biggest, burliest one on the line. Mostly, because of his size.

Don Victor said, "Number 6, say *why*?"

He might have been 6'7", Dominican, and reminiscent of a sasquatch, but he spoke like an ant. Formerly topping out around 300 flat, since all this started he'd lost close to 50 pounds on The Kappa Diet.

"I can't hear you," Don Victor said. "I said, say *why?*"

Number 6 gathered his strength, and spoke louder: "Why?"

"Why the fuck do you think?" Don Victor said, circling the entire line, like a shark. They'd try to remain stoic, The Brothers telling them they had to be strong and tight like a concrete wall. Nothing was to break them, nothing at all.

But Don Victor didn't give a fuck. He had seen it all.

"Because," he said, "that's what a man do. Because before anything else, a man stands, on his own two. And, if any one of you here cannot stand on your two? Then believe me. None of us here want you."

He continued: "And I got news for you, you skutch-ass niggas. All The Brothers around here? Look at them. Look around you, all of you. Look at them. Because, they want me to drop one of you."

The pledges believed him.

"They've been asking me all day," Don Victor said. "Trying to persuade me to finally, once and for all, as the founder of this Chapter, to get the fuck rid of one of you. Because, they want an example made. To everyone watching on campus, and especially to you—to your line—and to your line brothers at other Chapters—they want a message to get through. They want it to be known that we will accept no substitutes."

He paused.

Don Victor gathered himself.

"But, do you know what I told them? Do you know what I told them, you skutch-ass niggas?"

None of them answered.

Number 6 even put his head down.

"Pick your head up, God damn it," Don Victor said.

He did.

Don Victor went on, "And don't ever let me see you, don't ever let me see any of you, ever, in the course of your life ever stand or walk around with your head held down again."

He gave it a second…

"Because, if you do? You will not be Kappa men. Which leads me to what I told them. What I told these honorable, distinguished Brothers right here—pledges, I told them today not to drop any of you. Because I told them that you, all of you, as a unit—I told them that you've got potential. Motherfuckers, I told them that *I believe in you.*"

"So, again, I ask you: Why do you want to be Kappa men?"

The pledges thought about it. They thought about it hard, knowing full well what would happen if they gave the wrong answer. And for a minute, they went back and forth, whispering in each other's ears up and down the line like a game of telephone trying to find the right one.

They weren't allowed to speak out loud unless told to.

Once they thought they'd found it, the Number 1 stepped up. He took a step forward.

Don Victor asked, "Do you have something to say?"

The pledge nodded.

"Then, tell me, Number 1? Tell me… tell us… why do you want to be Kappa men?"

The Number 1 cleared his throat. He prepared himself.

And he said, with genuine sincerity:

"Because we need this."

Don Victor smiled.

But really, just because Don Victor didn't give a shit: "*Wrong answer!*"

BOOM.

The Brother in the back of the room *blasted* them with the fire hose.

THE PARTY

September, 1999

"So how we looking for tonight?" Red said, as they walked down the long, dingy, *gloomy* first floor hallway of The Kappa House. Which had been freshly mopped, and smelled lemon fresh for the first time all summer. Except now, summer was over. It was the first Friday of the school year, the one right before classes start.

"Everything's set," J.J. told him, his fellow Puerto Rican. "I posted the door schedules this morning."

"You feel good?"

"I feel great," J.J. said, wearing a fresh red shirt that read KAPPA across his chest in white letters, looking at the wooden plaques that lined the dark blue colored walls. Dark blue was the official Kappa color. And on most of those wooden plaques on the dark blue walls was a hand-made, hand-painted dedication to a different Brother. Others were made out to entire Lines. And some: to The Kappa Latino Fraternity as a whole.

In all, they were signs of Respect.

This was a house of Pride.

It felt good to be a Kappa.

"What I like to hear," Red said. "This is an important night. Matter of fact, this might just be, in some ways this is the most important night, of the entire year. Because, this is the night we set the example. The example every other night this year follows."

"This is the night we let the campus know who we are," J.J. said.

"Wrong."

"Huh?"

"They already know who we are. Now we remind them."

J.J. understood.

"But, don't get it twisted. We got to represent, J.J. But not just for us. And not just for The Kappa. For our ancestors. For our people. For everyone, for every migrant who ever plowed a field, hopped a fence, washed a dish or came over here on a raft. For everything we stand for, J.J. Do you understand?"

J.J. nodded his head.

"Good," Red said. "It's gonna be a good year."

"Our best."

"Let's hope so. How did flyering go last night?"

"We bombarded the campus," J.J. said.

"Any problems?"

"Nah, man. Diego and Klaw actually ran a train on a freshman."

"Already?"

"Tea bag and everything."

Red frowned at him.

J.J. shrugged his shoulders. "Like you said. It's gonna be a good year."

"Until one of us catches a rape charge. You got to put a stop to that, J.J."

"Red, we're students in college."

"Not you," Red said.

They stopped walking outside the bathroom door.

"Not me?" J.J. asked.

"Not at all," Red said, staring into his eyes. "Because, right now, you're more than just a student. Right now, you're my right hand. My vice president. Most likely making you the future president of the premier Chapter on this campus, not to mention one of the leading Chapters, if not *the* leading Chapter in this entire Fraternity, nation-wide. So, I'm telling you. I'm gonna tell you again, J.J. You need to represent. You got to step it up."

They heard the toilet flush.

They stared at the bathroom door.

Mario, The Dominican Sasquatch, all 6'7" and 300 pounds of his Chewbacca ass sauntered out of it followed by his stench in a beer stained undershirt and size 15 chancletas.

Even though he had a size 17 foot.

"Step it up for what?" he said, rubbing the crust out of his eyes, without having washed his hands. "Step it up for who?"

Red looked at him like dead weight. "For clowns like you. Look at you. What happened to you?"

Mario stretched.

He tried to crack his neck.

But—

He failed.

"I'm fucking stiff. I fell asleep, I passed out in the bathtub last night. Shit was crazy, son." He looked at J.J. "You remember that chick with the weave?"

Slowly, slightly—J.J. pushed open the bathroom door.

She was passed out on the floor.

Half-naked.

She *moaned*.

"That's all?" Red said.

"Nah, man." He looked at it: "Fucking bathtub."

It was littered with empty beer cans.

"I had a nightmare."

J.J. found it funny. "About what?"

"About what the fuck you think?" The Sasquatch bellowed, in his heavy baritone. "Pledging. The fucking fire hose."

"And why do you think that is?" Red said.

"I don't know, Red. You tell me. You're the one that approved it."

Red just looked at him. He tilted his head. "And why do you think that was?"

"Like I said. You tell me."

"Fine, Mario. It was because you weren't living up to your potential. Neither of you were. And, neither of you are now."

Mario rolled his eyes. "*Cabrón*." What he was hearing was wrong. "You know something… you need to lighten up, Red. Sometimes we wonder about you."

"And sometimes I wonder about your brain, Mario. What are you doing today?"

"We having the party."

"Not tonight," Red said. "*Today*."

"Oh," Mario said. "I got court."

"At what time?"

"One."

J.J. just looked at him: "Nigga: It's already two."

"Fuck!"

Mario was pissed off at himself.

Again.

"Look, Brothers," Red said. "You both know I consider you more than frat Brothers. I consider you real Brothers. Little Brothers. But, I'm a senior now. And y'all juniors. Which means you're getting older. So, let me just tell you this: You guys want to have nightmares about pledging? Brothers, you even want to dream about pledging anyone new? Then, you guys need to step it up. You guys need to represent. Mario, J.J.? Let me be clear: You need to lead the freshmen."

"I'm tired of this bullshit," Mario said, putting on fresh clothes, or whatever counted as fresh clothes in the big, wrinkled mess that was his room. A big Dominican flag hung across the wall. That was wrinkled, too.

"What bullshit exactly is it that you speak of?" J.J. said, sitting on the small couch in the corner, the one next to the sink, as Mario slid on his favorite Kappa shirt, a dark blue one what read KAPPA across its chest in white letters. "It's the first weekend of school," J.J. said. "Classes haven't even started yet."

"Like I give a fuck," Mario said. "We're juniors. We shouldn't have to go to campus to steal food."

"But, we're not stealing the food. Petey's stealing the food. And I don't even really consider it stealing. It's more like a work benefit."

"I don't give a fuck," Mario said. "We need to get some pledges to do this shit."

"Well, I'll tell you this much. If we're gonna get some pledges to fill up the fridge for us? They can't be no chumps."

"Meaning, what?"

"Meaning, it's true what Red was saying. I mean, everyone that came before us? We got big shoes to fill."

Mario looked at himself in the mirror. The one above his dresser. Then, he slapped on some cologne:

Two different kinds:

A drop of Curve.

A splash of Cool Water.

He raised his eyebrow:

He *winked*.

"So?" he said. "How are we going to fill them."

"With our secret weapon," J.J. said.

Mario turned to him: "El Metro?"

"The pimp-mobile," J.J. said, as they rolled through the rustbelt-shithole that was Downtown Valence on their way to the campus. The welfare hoes stared at them from the bus stop. Their certified hoopty with the jumping sound-system was unlike anything they'd ever heard. Riding shotgun, J.J. seemed to enjoy it. Mario, pressing on the gas pedal with his big toe, was used to it.

"Don't laugh," Mario said. "I pack mad hoes in this thing."

"I'm not talking about this thing," J.J. said. "I'm talking about the van Elvis is bringing us."

"Yeah, well, until that pervert actually brings it, this is what we're working with," Mario said, turning up the volume to mask the sound of the rusted, sagging exhaust pipe beneath his bumper.

Where on campus, Monica ignored the sounds of horny freshmen with new, braver identities trying to talk to her. A freshman herself, Monica Galán walked across Valence

University with a thorough South Bronx swagger. In part because she'd made it out of the hood. Now, looking forward to four years on what The State of New York had deemed their flagship, Division-1 school. To get in, you needed good grades. Or, an excuse and a scholarship. The Dominican project princess had all three. Sporting average height and tough skin with just the right amount of dark brown meat to grab on to, she was just like the beautiful campus: A state school marketed as a private one. If where The Kappa House was located was Downtown, *This is Uptown*, she thought, as her phone rang. She wondered who was calling her. Monica took the Nokia out of her pocket, and looked at the screen. It read: SCUMBAG

She smiled.

Stopped walking, and, feeling good to be one of the only students on campus she'd seen with a cell, picked up: "J.J., qué lo qué?"

"On our way to campus."

"Who?" Monica said.

"Me and Mario," J.J. said.

"So, what up?" she said. "We chilling?"

"Nah, I don't think so."

"Why not?" Monica asked.

"Why do you think?"

J.J. said, "Mario's got a warrant."

"What?"

"Plus we got a meeting, also. But, look. Do you know why I'm calling you?"

"I can only imagine," Monica said.

"To remind you," J.J. said.

"Remind me about what?"

"That I'm counting on you tonight, Monica. That we're all counting on you tonight, the whole Family. And, you need to pay tribute to it."

"J.J.," she said, confused, "what are you talking about?"

"Monica," J.J. said, as clear as possible, "tonight you are to bring as much un-deteriorated, un-demolished, un-herpe'd out freshmen pussy to the house as possible."

Monica stopped walking. She put her phone down at her side for a second. A creepy white-boy in a trench coat smiled at her. So, she lifted it back up.

"You there?" J.J. said.

"Yeah," Monica said. "But… I thought you said you wanted me to recruit some freshmen pledges for you instead?"

J.J. was caught off guard: "Why? You got some already?"

Ryan was one of those white-boys, the crazy, redneck kind from the middle of nowhere. He also had a 4-foot tall bong in his hand when he answered the door to his suite with a smile, and said, "What's up, Mexican?"

"What up, cracker?" Monica told him from the hallway of the old dorm. "They here?"

"Yeah, we were waiting for you," he said, ushering her inside. "We're about to light this up."

She looked at the smoker.

"Right here?" she said, as she walked into the common area with this maniac. "With *that?* What are you, crazy?"

"What are you talking about?"

"The smoke detector's gonna go off."

Ryan put his comforting arm around her.

"No, it's not. I disconnected it already."

Tommy and Roberto laughed on the couch.

Tommy, he was a half-breed. A rugged, half-Latin/half-white mutt from The City. One of those. Caught in between.

Roberto, he was more laid back. A ghetto Latino playboy. Or, so he claimed.

"Doesn't matter," Monica said. "I'm not staying too long anyway."

"Why? Where do *you* gotta be?" Tommy said.

"Word," Roberto said. "Classes haven't even started yet."

"And yet," Monica said, looking at the bong, "you're already going in. You're gonna fail out."

"Not me," Roberto said. "I don't really smoke like that."

"Neither do I," Monica said.

"I just drink," Roberto said.

"Neither do I," Monica said.

"So," Tommy asked, "what do you do?"

She smiled. "I use condoms. But, yo, we out to this party tonight or what?"

"My *neegas*," Diego said, walking out of the service entrance of the dining hall. That was how he pronounced *niggas*. Diego was just over five feet tall, straight off the boat from D.R. He didn't speak respectable English and didn't much want to, either. The only reason he'd come to the U.S. was for college so he could learn the best strategies to open up a proper string of bodegas. Or, at least that's what he said on his scholarship application. Truth was he was in Valence because he'd seen *Animal House* as a child and had delusions of grandeur more than anything else. But now, he just walked towards Mario's waiting, dark green, 4-door clunker pushing three big boxes stacked on a hand-truck that was almost as tall as him.

The trunk popped as J.J. stepped out of it. "Where's Petey?" he said.

Diego shook his head. "Petey sent me instead. Too much heat, meng."

"Yeah," J.J. said, "maybe because you brought a hand-truck."

"Look, meng," Diego said. "I didn't bring it. I took it."

"For what?"

"For us to use."

"Yeah, but for what?" J.J. said.

"For what you think?" Diego said. "To move the hoes around the house."

Mario said from behind the wheel, "We got to get some pledges for that."

J.J. shook his head. "Well, what'd you pick up at least?"

Diego smiled: "Dinner, meng. Dinner."

J.J. was angry: "How the fuck did you go all the way to the God damn dining hall with a God damn hand-truck and only come out with rice and beans?"

"They didn't have no platanos, meng," Diego said.

"Are you fucking kidding me?" J.J. said, as they drove back to the house.

"No, meng," Diego said, in the backseat, sitting behind him. "They were all out."

"Honestly, J.J." Mario said, "I'm surprised he even got that. I heard Petey was getting fired."

Diego shrugged his shoulders. "He is black, meng."

"Which means you should be grateful," J.J. said.

"No," Mario said. He looked at the little Dominican in the rearview. "It means you should have told me you were going to campus. I would have gone with you."

"Yeah, *okay*," Diego said. "I went out hunting *early* today."

"Fuck you trying to say, nigga?" Mario said.

"That you need to get the fuck out of the bathtub, meng. I had like five different hoes today I need The Kappa help with."

Mario thought about it. "What kind?"

Diego inhaled.

Then exhaled: "Lot of snow bunnies this time of year."

Mario's ears perked up. "They coming to the party tonight?"

"One," Diego said, "I'm sure of it."

J.J., not taking him serious, said, "Yeah, and just how exactly are you sure of it?"

"Hey," Diego said.

Very serious: "Penetration is 9/10's of the law, meng."

Mario was happy to hear it.

J.J. couldn't believe it.

"What did she look like?" Mario said.

"Like someone we could run the train on, meng."

J.J. shook his head again.

"You know what?" J.J. said.

"What's up, J.J.?" Diego said.

J.J. said, "Red was right. Matter of fact, Red is always right. This has to stop."

Diego, concerned, slid left to the middle of the seat. Turned his head to the right, and looked at him in shotgun: "Fuck you talking about?"

"Diego," J.J. said, "we are students at a top tier university. A Division-1 school. And we got the opportunities that Latinos all over the world would die for. Have died for. So, we got to, we have to focus. On what's important. On building for the future, building for our people. So, we have to, we have to step it up. Red is right. Red is *so* right."

He continued: "Diego... we have to be that example."

Diego smirked. "Well check out this example right here, Bro." He took two Polaroid pictures of the fat white chick from that morning out of his pocket: "She let me take her pictures, meng."

"So you really got a full scholarship, huh?" Tommy said as the smoke poured out of the bong.

"In high school I was All-American," Ryan said, cradling his lacrosse stick in his hands.

"In Kentucky?" Tommy said, coughing out the words through the weed smoke.

"That's right," Ryan said, taking in his new surroundings. Next to his bong, his gas-mask, the smoke detector and an ounce of Kentucky Kush were on the coffee table. Which really livened up the place. Their suite wasn't in one of the brand new buildings the campus had just built, instead in one of the old ones on the list to be refurbished. So, it all evened out. Monica and Roberto lived upstairs on the 2nd and 3rd floors of the old 3-story dorm. Tommy and Ryan were roommates in a 3-bedroom, 6-man suite on the ground level.

Which to Ryan meant paradise: "I grew up in a fucking trailer park."

Tommy felt bad for him. "You have roaches and shit in there?"

"Hell, no," Ryan said, taking a hit off the bong. "My pops was the landlord. Good money in degenerates."

"Tell me about it," Monica said.

"Why?" Tommy asked. "Where'd *you* come from?"

"The projects," Monica said.

"In The Bronx?" Ryan said.

She corrected him: "In The South Bronx."

"So, what up, then?" Roberto said. "What's the deal with this party tonight? You really know these niggas?"

"I grew up with them," Monica said. "Some of them, anyway."

Roberto asked, "And their house is sick?"

"I mean…" Monica smiled. "It's the only one on campus that has a pool. Only one I know of at least. You should come through. I'm telling you, you'll like them."

"So, I run into this chick in the hallway," Diego said, "in the Cayuga building. I was about to slide the party flyer for tonight under her door… but then, she opened it. And I look up. And she's standing there, staring right at me, wearing nothing but a big, fat, giant, teddy bear." He lowered his voice: "And I'm telling you, she looked ripe, meng. Like a peach fry."

"With Adobo on top?" Mario asked.

As the two of them and J.J. mixed up drinks in eight big red and blue Gatorade coolers with big wooden spoons in the old, rusty kitchen for the fiesta that night. All around them was an array of filth, cobwebs, pineapples, limes, oranges, sugar, berries, a small Ziploc bag full of e-pills and enough cheap vodka to keep it going past the break of dawn.

As Klaw, their fellow junior and Chinese Line Brother in his dark blue Kappa baseball jersey that said KLAW on the back above the number 4 in gold lettering tried to understand what Diego was talking about while he cooked dinner for the house on the beat up stove and the George Foreman grill sitting next to it. With an accent reminiscent of a ghetto Bruce Lee, he asked, "What do you mean, *ripe*, Diego?"

"I mean, so ripe, meng," Diego said, "that she could go to NYU. *Business*, meng."

J.J. looked at him like he was crazy. "What the fuck does that even mean?"

Diego wasn't exactly sure. "I don't know, meng. But, she was fat, and I thought she would look better in a suit. All white people look better in a suit. I love a nice hip-bones to grab on to."

The rest of them had no idea where he was going with this.

Klaw tilted his head. Turned away from the giant cauldron of rice and beans on the stove, and towards J.J. and Mario, saying: "It feels good to be back, man. After 9 months abroad, it feels damn good. Home sweet home, hermanos."

"You enjoyed your trip though, right?" Mario said.

"You kidding me, man? *Muchacho*." It was The Kappa way of saying *Jesus Christ*. "I ran with the bulls."

"Táto," Mario said. "What I like to hear."

"If only I wish I could hear the same," Klaw said.

"What's that mean?" Diego said.

"It means, Diego... Mario... I hear you two got sent to The Valence County Jail. Qué fue, hermanos? Qué páso, man?"

"My nigga," Mario said, "nobody told you?"

"I was abroad, man. But, I been back 24 hours, and I hear all these crazy stories... and, I have to be honest."

"What?" Mario said. "You trying to pass judgment?"

"*Muchacho*," Klaw said again. "No. If anything, regretment."

Diego looked at him: "Huh?"

"Because," Klaw said, "I wish I was there."

"In the jail?" J.J. asked.

"Of course in the jail," Klaw said.

"With these two idiots?" J.J. looked at Diego and Mario. Then, back at Klaw. He thought he was nuts: "Why?"

"Why do you think?" Klaw said. "I heard it was fun, man."

Mario looked at him: "They did have good boloney sandwiches, bro."

Red and J.J., boss and underboss at the head of the second floor living room looked around proud at what they'd built. Or at least, *confident*. 17 of their 20 active Brothers all dressed in unison as a team, a functioning cadre, a unit in preparation for the night's festivities. Every one of them now had on their dark blue Kappa baseball jerseys, all with the gold lettering on them. Seated there in the living room with the dark blue painted walls like a Family under more wooden plaques and a giant KAPPA flag eating a hearty meal of rice, beans, and a case of stolen tuna seasoned with Adobo. Then again, everything they made was seasoned with Adobo. J.J.'s also had some balsamic vinegar on the side. He was that kind of guy. They all had slices of lime.

"I didn't get to pledge you," Klaw said to Manveed, sitting on one of the couches. They didn't have a big enough table to seat them all in one place. Well, they did, but Diego and Mario and this thick heffer broke it. So, for the time being, they all had their plates in their laps. Klaw said, "You're lucky."

"Your loss," Manveed told him, adjusting his turban. "I got my Hindu on."

"And I got my guerilla on," Carlos said, with his Colombian accent. "These skutch-ass niggas loved me, Klaw."

Manveed rolled his eyes in acknowledgment. "It would have been nice if you'd said that at some point."

Carlos smiled: "Actions speak louder than words, Brother." He turned to his Chinese contemporary: "Klaw, you would have loved it." His face lit up. "I made them an obstacle course."

Klaw nodded his head in approval. He was proud. "Where, hermano?"

"At the Lakota reservation," Carlos said. "They let me borrow it."

"They let you *borrow* it?"

"Like in the old country."

"Did you give it back at least?"

"With new tools," Carlos said, as he took a bite. "And some skills."

A fellow junior/Line Brother, before he came to the U.S. for college Carlos was an ex-child soldier in the jungles just outside Medellín in Colombia, giving birth to his Line Name. On the back of Carlos' baseball jersey, above his number, 5, read: GUERILLA.

On the back of Mario's, above the number 6: SASQUATCH.

Carlos went on: "I taught them some tricks, Bro. Some strategies. They're a smarter people now." Then looked at Manveed and Slinky (J.J.'s dumb, weasel of a sophomore half-brother who pledged with the Hindu in Carlos' death traps and war camps). He said: "I love y'all niggas, fam."

Slinky put his head down. He was still traumatized.

Manveed didn't give a fuck. He couldn't wait to pledge someone else instead.

Red prepared his words. He cleared his throat.

"Brothers," he said, as they cleaned their plates. They always cleaned their plates. No morsels were left behind. An aftereffect of what being starved by a gun-toting Colombian maniac like *The Guerilla* could do to you.

"Brothers," Red said, standing up. "Let's begin."

He moved to the middle of the room. It might have been old, the floors and walls creaky, weak and thin, but, it was quite spacious, just enough for The Chapter to fill it up.

"Brothers," Red said, surveying the captive audience, feeling them out. Because, the truth was, none of them ever had a desire to listen to his Kappa speeches and campus manifestos. However, each and every Brother in that room had an undying respect for Red. So, they gave him their full attention. Except Mario, who J.J. slapped upside the head.

"Well," Red said, "the truth is, as your Chapter president, I'm not really sure how to begin this meeting... So, let me just start, by saying:"

"That you're all a bunch of twats," Manveed replied.

Or, interrupted as the whole room broke out in laughter.

"You should have seen this Hindu ass nigga," Carlos told Klaw. "India got heart."

"Anyone seen Hidalgo?" Diego asked, generally curious.

"Man, fuck Hidalgo," Mario said. "Fuck that spiritual maricón."

"*Brothers*," Red said, louder, stronger this time.

The room came to order.

Red paused.

He said: "Look, Brothers. I know you're all anxious for tonight. And I know this is an important night. But, for me, as our Chapter president, it's important to me to say a few things right now before this year officially starts."

Red looked around the room.

He locked eyes with J.J.

Then, began again: "So, Brothers... Before we hit The Kappa Signal? Right now, I just want all of you to do one thing for me. Brothers, right now, I want all of us to be serious. On the same page, professional, just for a moment. Because, as we start this new semester? I want us all to have clear heads. Clear minds. So we can keep something in mind: Our history. And, do any of you know why?"

No one answered.

Red went on, "Because, even though we like to party, crack jokes and all, let's remember that we are not just some other Latino fraternity. No. In fact, we are not like *any* of the other Latino fraternities out there. So, we must not carry ourselves like any of the other dumb, stupid, jive-ass fraternities out there. Because, unlike every other Latino fraternity out there? Us, we, *The Kappas?* Brothers, we don't just go back to a pledge process.

Brothers, we go back to The Lautaro Lodge. To something, *real*. To something, *historical*. So, just remember this... With whatever you do this year? With whatever class you take? With, frankly, whatever hoe you fuck."

Diego smiled: "Meng."

"Brothers," Red said, "never forget that our ancestors fought, and bled, and died and gave their hearts out for us to be here today. To be here, tonight, in this place. For us to be, to be able to be, here, members of The Latino Fraternity Among Latino Fraternities. So, no matter what we do this year? Let us be proud. And, confident. But, humble, and *never* cocky. Because, what happens when you get cocky?"

The room went silent.

Manveed took a shot: "You get laid?"

"No," Red said. "You get sloppy. And the minute we forget that—

Slinky, the weasel, raised his hand.

Red looked at him: "Yes, Slinky?"

"I got a question, Red."

"I can see that."

But, Slinky didn't ask it.

Red just continued to stare at him.

Then, the whole room stared at him.

He wasn't that bright.

Red rolled his eyes: "Okay, Slinky. Go ahead."

"Red, my question is, how can you be humble, when you're the king of the jungle?"

"Well, luckily for yourself," Red said, "you don't have to worry about that."

"Petey!" J.J. said, happy to see him. His lazy, Black, fellow Line Brother who just happened to be a Muslim entered the room with a big cardboard box in his hands and a dark blue kufi on his bald head. It said KAPPA on it in off-white letters.

"You're late," Red said.

Petey brushed it off: "I was in The Dining Hall, kid."

Red looked at him: "So?"

"What's in the box?" Mario asked.

"Chicken wings, chicken wings," Petey said. "Motherfucking chicken wings."

"Brothers," Red said. "Your attention."

Petey looked around, realizing the Chapter meeting he'd walked into. "My bad, fellas."

He sat down. "Proceed."

"Look," Red said. "You guys all know I love to speak. But, you also know, this is my last year here, my last year as president, and so, in not too long from now it's going to be time for a new generation to step up."

Red stopped, and looked around.

Then, continued:

"So, with that… I'm going to pass the mic."

He looked at J.J.

They made eye contact, and Red gave him the nod.

Red stepped aside, and after a second, J.J. stepped up.

"Thanks," J.J. said.

Truth be told, J.J. was honored.

So, he took a moment.

Then, got into it:

"Well, you know, it's true what Red was saying. What Red is always saying."

They locked eyes again.

J.J.'s attention went back to The Chapter:

"And, I mean, I mean that, Brothers. Because, this right here? Brothers, this ain't just no ordinary, college, whatever the fuck, Latino Greek Fraternity Chapter. Brothers, this right here? This right here, this is progress. This is an achievement, man. Because, let's be serious. With the, with the semester of '96, with the suspension, with everything that came before right now? Let's be for real. Brothers, there were plenty of times when no one thought we'd make it this far. Yet, here we are."

"Running shit," Carlos said.

"Word," J.J. said. "But, it's also true, that the minute we get sloppy? That's the minute this whole thing of ours right here falls apart. That's the minute someone else takes our place. And, yo? All them campesinos coming over here hopping fences right now? All those dishwashers and doormen who would do anything just to have a chance? Believe you and me, they wish it was *their* kids in our shoes. They wish it was *them* living in this house right here."

Slinky, staring at the cracks in the ceiling, and feeling the weak floorboard beneath his feet, was confused: "But, J.J?"

"What?"

"This house is a piece of shit," Slinky said.

"So what?" J.J. said. "It's *our* piece of shit. And, this lifestyle? This lifestyle right here? This is The American Dream, Brothers. But, whatever you do? Whatever you do, do not take it for granted. Because, in a few short years? In no time at all? I'm telling you, there's going to be more Latinos in this country than anything else."

Nobody knew what to say to that.

But, Diego had a question.

He was concerned.

He looked around, and asked:

"Then, what does that mean, *for us*?"

"Well," J.J. said. Taking his time. He caught his breath: "It's going to be hard to get a landscaping job."

"And run trains on virgins," Manveed said, as the whole Chapter laughed, imagining a future with one too many lawn mowers.

Diego looked at him: "Not they fat ones, meng."

J.J. smiled.

He looked at Red.

Even Red smiled.

"Look, fellas," J.J. said, "we got the whole year to do workshops. So, all, please rise."

Everyone did.

They all stood up, into a circle around J.J., their vice-president, and the guy they all knew was one day going to be one of The Kappa's most esteemed leaders.

"Because," J.J. said, "let me just tell you this. Because, unlike what Red said? No. Sorry. I got news for you, Brothers."

He continued, "Brothers, we are not members of The Latino Fraternity Among Latino Fraternities."

Red asked, "We're not?"

"We're not," J.J. said. "Not at all. Because, Brothers? Brothers, we are members of The Chapter Among Chapters in The Latino Fraternity Among Latino Fraternities, and it's up to us, right now, in the name of all of our ancestors who were not able to be here and experience this and go through all the cueros that we're going to run through this year to make our college experience The Best Chapter of our lives."

They all agreed. The whole room nodded their heads.

"So," J.J. said, "Brothers, let's start this year off with a bang. And tonight, like every other opening night, let's set the bar high." J.J. paused… "And, why are we going to set the bar high?"

The entire Chapter looked around at each other.

Then, chanted together:

"'CAUSE WE'RE KAPPA TO DEATH, DO OR DIE!"

With their arms around each other in a circle kind of like a Dominican mosh pit even though they were not all Dominican they all started jumping, up, down, jumping around and celebrating and STOMPING their boots on the ground as they YELLED:

"HEY! HEY! HEY! HEY! HEY! HEY! HEY! HEY!"

BUT: Mario, with his size 17 foot, currently wearing a size 18 Timberland boot stomped TOO hard and his giant hoof *crashed* through the weak floor board, twisted his ankle as Diego looked on in horror, wincing in extreme pain and falling over to the side taking Brothers with him like dominoes, crashing into plates of food and spilling cups of Kappa juice everywhere as the whole House *shook*.

Mario *screamed*.

It might have been broken.

"Ahhhhhhhhhhhhhhhhh!!!!!!!!!!!!"

Valence County Cops Officer Graham and Sergeant Lopresti heard the shout all the way from the undercover Plymouth up the block, almost from the other side of the dead end, where they were eating pizza-donuts and staking out The Kappa House.

They watched its lights flicker as it shook.

"That enough for probable cause?" Officer Graham asked, the oil from the pizza-donut dripping on his shirt.

"On what grounds?" Sergeant Lopresti said.

"I don't know. Unsafe living conditions? We could always condemn the place."

"And have their landlord make a beef down at the hall? I don't think so." Sergeant Lopresti shook his head. "The one thing you don't want, *rookie*, is a problem with Vincent LoScalzo's wife."

Officer Graham understood where he was coming from.

"And besides," Sergeant Lopresti said, "all they'd do is move to some other flophouse anyway."

"Okay. But, then, what do we do?"

"We wait," Sergeant Lopresti said, turning his head to his junior officer. Giving him a confident, evil smile. He pinched Officer Graham's cheek. "We wait."

"We wait?"

"Don't worry, pal," Sergeant Lopresti said. "Even if it takes the whole, entire semester, we'll get them. These fucking beaners are out of rice and they don't even know it yet."

"Elvis," Monica said, picking up her phone, inside Tommy's suite. "What the deal, Turkey? You there?"

"Turkey?" Tommy asked, about to pre-game a shot of dirt cheap vodka with Roberto and Ryan, in addition to some short Chinese sluts from down the hall.

"Elvis?" Ryan said, chasing his with some kind of knock-off soda concoction. "What is this guy, the king of cabs?"

"Táto," Monica said. "We'll be outside."

"Elvis the king," Elvis said, with his perverted, middle-aged Turkish lisp as the Turkish gypsy music pumped off the speakers inside his old, used, decked out Chevy Astro-Van as they zipped through the downtrodden streets of Downtown Valence. "Elvis the king, that's what they call me," he said. It was even written over a big crown on the sides and back of his Astro-Van. Which was dark blue, primarily because he was a Kappa fan. He said, "In Valence, everybody know me. All the teachers, they love me. Ask your friend. I give them my cucumbers, man."

Tommy, in the back with Monica and Roberto, on the vomit stained seat that was highlighted by the blue neon interior lights found all this hilarious. He said: "You're my hero, Elvis."

"For real," Roberto followed, enjoying the music.

Elvis loved it.

He may not have loved the extra layer of falafel around his waist these days or even the pattern of whiteheads piercing through his undershirt on his hairy upper back, but, he did love his gypsy music. It reminded him of home. "You just listen to me," he said, steering like a slow Speed Racer. "You listen to me, and you be the pimp number one at the U of V. I promise."

"We believe you," Tommy said.

Roberto asked, "So how many years you been out here, fam?"

"I come from Turkey 5 years ago," Elvis said. "So, you need anything, I get the discount."

"Discount?" Roberto was perplexed.

"I got a guy," Elvis said.

"What about information?" Roberto said. "Can you get us information?"

"Like the internet?" Elvis asked. "I'm on there too, my friend. I got a page on MiGente. Two of them, to be exact."

"What?" Tommy laughed.

"That's my shit," Elvis said. "Salvadorian bitches, they love me. But, I got one for the snowflakes, also. It's on AOL."

"Got to," Monica said.

"That's not what I meant," Roberto told him. "I mean, that's what up, for real for real, but, uh, nah." He laughed. "Not what I meant."

"So, talk to me, then," Elvis said. "What's the confusion?"

Roberto said, "No confusion. I was just asking about, like, this house we're going to. What's the deal with the people who live there?"

"You didn't ask your friend here?" Elvis said.

"They want an unbiased source," Monica told him.

"Hey," Elvis said, "all I know is The Kappa are good peoples, man. I give them free rides and they get me free pussies."

"Really?" Tommy asked.

Roberto furrowed his brow.

"100 percent," Elvis said, shooting some saliva out through his lisp.

Monica agreed: "It's true."

"All the time," Elvis told them. "I put my cucumber in them, man. Pimps. But, wait till you see their house."

"We heard they got a pool," Tommy said.

"With a mansion," Roberto followed.

Elvis was thrown off by this.

In response, he just looked at Monica in the rearview:

"A mansion?"

She shrugged.

Elvis braced himself.

He even pulled over.

For the first time all night, he turned down the music, and turned to his disciples in the back seat. Elvis told them, "That place ain't no mansion, fellas. That place is haunted."

Tommy said, "Haunted?"

"Haunted," Elvis said. "Used to be a funeral parlor. I'm talking spirits and shit."

"So, what you think?" Carlos said, standing with J.J. outside the front door, as bouncers. With Carlos looking up, at The Kappa Signal in the sky. You know, like The Bat Signal, except the spotlight in their backyard just blasted the word KAPPA into the heavens. Letting everyone in Valence know it was going down at The Kappa House.

J.J. had other things on his mind. He said, "I'm thinking, I'm happy to be a Kappa, and, I'm happy to be living in this giant, gigantic, used-to-be of a castle, but explaining to Mrs. LoScalzo how Mario's foot went through the floor is going to be a pain in the ass."

"Like it's our fault."

"Like she's not a psycho."

"Like we couldn't sue."

"Like if we did she couldn't have us whacked."

"Yeah, but like that don't work both ways," Carlos said. "You come from The Bronx, and I come from Colombia. Don't forget, Pablo paid for my house. Don't be scared of those guinea motherfuckers."

"Alright," J.J. said. "But, then, where does that leave us?"

"Truth be told, I don't understand, hermano. Her husband runs this town, at least all the construction in it."

"And she has his balls in a sling. I gotta be honest, though."

"About what?"

"I kind of wish she was a guy so we could recruit her," J.J said. As a troop of ladies, Latin girls, certified brown-skinned sorority sluts walked up to the creepy, monstrous ghetto mansion. They could hear the music thumping through the walls from all the way down the street.

"What's the word, J.J.?" Estefania, the head hoe said. "Carlos. How's it hanging, fellas?"

"Straight down the middle," Carlos said. "I got the macheté. Want to see?"

"I want to see Mario, tell you the truth."

"Why?" J.J. asked.

"That nigga owes me forty dollars. He never returned my textbook. And Monica, too, where she at?"

"Why?" J.J. asked again. "She in the hole as well?"

Carlos opened the massive, gold-painted, 11-foot high front door for them. It was heavy, even for him. And he was ripped, from years of jungle guerilla training.

As the girls went inside, and the ocean of reggaeton music poured out, Estefania said, "If she gets on line. You know how that go."

"Yeah, okay," J.J. said.

"Okay, what?" Estefania said.

J.J. said, "Okay, what I know is that if you try to pledge my little sister she's gonna hand your ass to you."

"We'll see about that," Estefania said, as the door closed behind her.

Carlos asked J.J., "You believe that?"

"Believe what?"

"That fool owes her forty dollars? For a textbook? *That* nigga had a textbook?"

"Look, Carlos," J.J. said. "You can call him a nigga, but I'm not you sure should call him a fool."

"I shouldn't?"

"Nah," J.J. said. "He sold it to Diego for fifty."

"I'm gonna bust this asshole, too," Sergeant Lopresti said, watching Elvis' Astro-Van fishtail around the corner onto the long dead end from the undercover Plymouth.

"Why?" Officer Graham said. "What'd *he* do?"

"He's a scout for them, for their whole operation."

"The girls?" Officer Graham said.

"The girls, the liquor, everything," Sergeant Lopresti said.

Graham ate another pizza-donut.

"And I'll tell you this: 20 bucks says he don't got his papers."

Not like Elvis cared. He didn't. Not real ones, anyway. But, the ones The Kappas got him passed the test. So, as Elvis clipped the corner, Elvis turned the music up. Not from inside the van, but the custom speaker he had built on the outside, like an ice cream truck, so everyone could hear him coming. From what he could tell there was a crowd of about 20 people in front of The Kappa House and The King had to make an entrance.

"J.J., my boy," Elvis said.

J.J. shook his hand through the front window at the curb.

He eyed the peanut gallery in the back. He said: "Elvis. Monica. Friends of Monica."

"Hey," Elvis said, as the freshmen got their money out, "the friends of The Kappa are also the friends of mine."

They paid him, and thanked him.

"No problem," Elvis said. "Just tell your friends that if they need ride, I'm that guy."

"You got it, boss," Tommy said.

"Word," Roberto said, stepping out of the cab, looking up at the massive, dark blue Kappa House with the gold-painted front door in awe. At the three stories, the three gigantic stories and the odd shape of it. At the imposing gold-painted KAPPA sign on the front of it.

This was not what Roberto expected. Monica undersold this place. When Tommy tapped him on the shoulder and motioned to The Kappa Signal in the sky they hadn't noticed from inside the van, Roberto just thought, *What the fuck?*

Tommy smiled. "This is awesome."

Roberto turned back to the driver and said, "You cool peoples, Elvis."

"Word," Tommy said. "Thanks for bringing us."

"Good," Elvis said. "You just make sure you tell everybody over there that. Especially, *her*." He pointed at some girl in the crowd. "I think she's an Indian."

"East Indian, actually," J.J. said. "Sophomore. Want me to bring her over?"

Elvis thought about it… "Nah, next time. I got dollars to make."

J.J. said, "No doubt, partner."

"Speaking of which," Elvis said, through his disgusting lisp, "where's Mario? I don't see Mario. Where's the bigfoot?"

"Word," Monica said. "Don't he usually do the door?"

"He's, uh…" J.J. smiled. "In the floor."

"Okay," Elvis said. "Tell him then I said what up."

"Will do," J.J. said.

"I know," Elvis said. "That's my nigga. We run a train together."

With that, Tommy and Roberto's attention was diverted from the house of ratchet before them. They turned to him, to Elvis, wanting to hear more.

Elvis said, "Here, J.J., I got you," reaching into the glove compartment. He took out two pictures and gave them to him. "What I was telling you about."

J.J. looked at the pictures.

His eyes lit up. They were of an old, 18-passanger Econoline van.

"Yeah," J.J. said, "this is nice. Exactly what we were looking for."

Because it was beat half to death, a real piece of shit, one step away from being destroyed. Making it cheap, and one good paintjob, a body kit and an oil change away from making them The K-Team.

"Okay," Elvis said. "But, do you got what *I'm* looking for?"

J.J. smiled.

He whistled at Carlos. Nodded at him to open the front door. Two minutes later Black Petey walked out with two ghetto fabulous prostitutes on his arms, black chicks, two of Valence's finest whores.

On the sideline Tommy and Roberto looked on in amazement as Elvis, excited, stepped out of the taxi in front of the small crowd rubbing his hands together as Petey walked these two fine sub-human specimens towards the car. One of them was in a short fake-fur skirt.

Elvis looked at it. Looked both of them up and down. Like *a creep*, through his lisp, he said: "Hello, *ladies*."

The one in the fake-fur smiled.

Through the space between her gold teeth, she told him: "Hello, *Turkey*."

They entered a new world. Outside it was somewhat quiet, the soundproofed walls—okay, the first floor windows covered with foam and cardboard and all kinds of shit, rather masked what inside was like the secret party in The Catskills from *Dirty Dancing*. Times 1,000, with brown people.

Students were having sex, everywhere, only with their clothes on. As J.J. walked Monica, Tommy and Roberto through the swamp, what the Brothers called their enormous first floor dance floor with the 20-foot high ceiling when it got packed, sweaty and muggy like it was now. You could get lost in it.

There must have been over 200 people in there.

And it was early. Things hadn't even gotten started yet.

The crowd got down to a thick reggaeton. But Tommy had never heard reggaeton before. He'd never seen a Dominican midget dancing with his face in a girl's ass-crack, either.

College, he thought.

It was wet and steamy, the raunchiest party Tommy and Roberto had ever seen. Rump-shaking was an understatement, you could hardly breathe. In every direction unabashed Latino college kids were grinding all over each other. But, that wasn't what had Tommy's attention.

Mesmerized, he looked toward the top of the walls. Around the room, just below the ceiling were a series of dark blue Kappa baseball jerseys like the ones The Brothers were wearing now, except framed in glass cases like they were in the hall of fame. One of them, which read VICTOR on the back in gold above the number 7, stood out.

It was featured prominently.

Seeing Tommy taking it all in, J.J. asked them, "So, you guys liking college so far?"

"I don't know," Roberto said, barely hearing him above the noise. "Is this how it is every day out here?"

J.J. said, a little louder, "Not really. The hoes don't usually show up till around one. Come on though, I'll give you a tour."

Entering the first floor hallway the first thing Tommy and Roberto noticed were the three Brothers at the foot of a narrow staircase, drinking, but looking up the 30 steps to the second floor like they were waiting for something to happen.

They weren't from Valence, though. They were from the Syracuse Chapter. J.J. asked them, "Any victims, yet?"

The Syracuse Brothers didn't say nothing. They figured by the way J.J. was escorting Tommy and Roberto that he was recruiting them. Especially since he met them by way of Monica, who was Family to him. Guiding them through the dense hallway traffic though, seeing Tommy and Roberto look at the plaques that lined the walls—and the sexy freshman bitches that walked in their direction back towards the dance floor—they arrived at the bar.

A five-foot-high, pledge-made wet bar placed in front of the entrance to the kitchen. It was painted white and said KAPPA on it in dark blue. On top were two of the Gatorade coolers, a red one and an official-colored one. Behind it unsmooth Slinky served drinks in red plastic cups.

Tommy was surprised. He said, "You don't got kegs?"

J.J. told him, "White people got kegs. Guys, this is my little Brother, Slink."

"Your blood brother or your frat brother?" Roberto asked.

"Both," Slinky said. "We got a cousin in The Chicago Chapter though, also. What's poppin', homies?"

"What up, man?" Roberto said.

"Y'all freshmen?" Slinky sized them up. "I could tell." He got them two cups, and said, "Try this right here, fellas."

"What is it?" Tommy asked.

"In this cooler we got Kappa Punch," J.J. said, referring to the blue one. "And in this one, we got Nutcrackers."

"Like in The City?" Roberto said, impressed.

Nutcracker was a modern day moonshine, sold out of backrooms, pool halls, barber shops, even in bodegas and out of minivans parked on street corners across parts of Upper Manhattan and The South Bronx.

And now, out of The Kappa House.

"Exclusive," Slinky said.

Roberto smiled. "That's what's up, yo."

J.J. told them, motioning to the sign that spelled it out, "The juices is free, just like admission. But we got shots of Cuervo, too, a dollar each."

Slinky poured them two cups of Kappa Punch to start off and, seeing that they found it delicious, J.J. said, "Any other time you need that, we could put it in a bottle for you, five dollars a piece."

These guys were bootleggers.

Tommy and Roberto liked what they heard.

So did Monica. Red came up behind her and said, "Dímelo, mujer."

She was happy to see him: "What's the word, Red?"

"Them Gamma girls is around here, somewhere, looking for you. Estefania, she was asking about you."

"That slut?" Monica said. "What'd she want?"

"She asked how you were."

"What'd you tell her?"

Red said, "That you're a freshman in college."

Then, he eyed Tommy and Roberto. He said: "Who this?"

"I got it," J.J. said. "Red, this is Tommy and Roberto. They live in Monica's building, on campus. Guys, this is Red. He's our Chapter President."

"Oh," Roberto said, giving respect. "Well, then it's very nice to meet you."

"No problem," Red said.

"What?" Roberto asked.

Red asked back, "Y'all from The B.X. also?"

"Nah," Tommy said, "I'm from Queens."

All these Uptown dudes were foreign to him.

Not Roberto. He told him, with pride: "I'm from Harlem, yo. Spanish Harlem."

J.J. acknowledged, "There's a lot of bitches over there."

"Yeah, I know," Monica said. "And half of them are pregnant."

"Monica!" Klaw said, pronouncing her name in a way Bruce Lee would have been proud. He popped up out of nowhere, covered in sweat.

"Dance partner!" she told him, happy to see him. They *hugged.* She asked, "How are you!? How was your trip!?"

"Please," Klaw said. "You know Kappas. It doesn't matter where we are. We're going to make it happen, *regardless.*"

"Yeah," she told him. "Tell that to Immigration."

On the side Tommy asked J.J., "You guys got Chinese Brothers?"

"We got all kinds of Brothers," Red said.

J.J. nodded. "Indians, too. Yo, Klaw."

"Yo?" Klaw said.

J.J. showed him the pictures:

"The van, that Elvis is giving us."

Klaw got excited: "Oh, this is hot."

"I know," J.J. said, "we'll hook this thing up."

Red told them, "Why don't you go show those to Mario? You'll make his night."

As Monica asked, "What happened to Mario?"

The music switched—from reggaeton to merengue. It was fast paced; it had a heavy drumbeat. Now, Klaw got *really* excited. His shoulders, then his hips started to move. He said, "Oh, this is my song, Bro." He looked at her: "Monica!"

She smiled. "*Bailar.*"

He grabbed her hand. They took off for the dance floor.

Which confused young Tommy: "He could dance, too?"

J.J. told him, "Don't judge a book by its cover."

"But," Tommy said, "he's Chinese?"

"Actually," Red said, "he's Colombian."
J.J. agreed: "He grew up in Medellín."

If there was one difference between the Latin and white parties in Valence… or, one difference between the Latin and any other types of parties in Valence… it was that, while people at the other parties might have wanted to dance—the people at the Latin parties *knew* how to dance.

And at The Kappa House parties in particular, they danced *hard*. It got wild. But even so—the entire dance floor gave Klaw and Monica their space. Growing up in Colombia, Klaw had to fight to prove he was the best dancer in the barrio. Meaning that when he got to Valence, he established with ease that he was the strongest dancer at the school. In addition to being the finest speaker of his native tongue. His *er* verbs were flawless.

In amazement, Tommy and Roberto looked on from near the foot of the first floor staircase where they had a perfect view of Monica and Klaw tearing it up.

"So," Roberto asked, "what other countries you got Brothers from?"

"New Jersey," J.J. said.

"New Jersey?" Tommy responded.

J.J. gave it a moment. Then, told them, "Look, I'm not gonna lie to you. We're not like other frats. And honestly, we're not even a frat. Not primarily at least. But, we got Brothers from everywhere, man."

The Syracuse Brothers, kicking game to some cueros and admiring the pictures of the future Kappa-Mobile, agreed.

J.J., though, peeping the freshman at the top of the 30 narrow steps, about to come down, with a red plastic cup in his hand and chugging what was left in it, told them, "Watch this."

The kid didn't make it till the fifth when he lost his balance, his right foot went out from under him and he slid down the liquor and sweat covered steps on his ass like it was a sled.

He held his gluts at the bottom of them, in dire need of an icepack.

J.J. looked at him. Then, at Tommy and Roberto, and shook his head. "Every time. There's always someone. Be careful."

They were, and upon reaching the second floor joined a whole different scene. Nowhere near as intense as the first, because if the first floor was the nightclub, this was the lounge. Students played beer pong in a space near the kitchen, others played on the foosball table in a corner. Nobody was playing their *Street Fighter* arcade game but two cute girls played *NBA JAM* on the machine next to it and two others played *Teenage Mutant Ninja Turtles* on the one next to that one. And every here and there, a Kappa Brother stood guard doing security.

Looking into the big second floor living room, however, which was closed off by yellow police tape, Tommy and Roberto saw the orange traffic cone stationed over the spot where Mario's immense boot went through the floor.

"Trust me," J.J. said, "you don't want to go in there."

After seeing the mishap on the stairs, they took his word for it. But, Roberto asked him, "What did you mean before?"

"About what?" J.J. said.

"About you guys, you know, not really being a frat?"

J.J. was about to answer him.

Instead, he changed his mind and approached a Brother standing guard in front of a closed door, making sure no one opened it, and said, "Yo, you seen Mario?"

"He's upstairs," the Brother said. "In the V.I.P. room."

J.J. asked, "Doing what?"

"Doing what you think? El Metro."

J.J. found it funny. Like an inside joke.

J.J. turned to the freshmen, and said: "Look. Talking to Elvis? I can only imagine what you must have heard."

"In all honesty?" Roberto said. "Talking to Monica, too?"

Tommy told him, "We heard that most fraternities are stupid."

J.J. agreed. "They are."

"So," Roberto said, "what makes yours different?"

J.J. smiled. "I could tell you. Or, I could show you."

The Brother opened the door he was guarding to reveal a narrow, used-to-be-hidden staircase, like something out of The Underground Railroad.

Or, in this case, a speakeasy/bordello during Prohibition.

It led them up to the third floor, which was different than the others. This one was empty. It was V.I.P. only, almost quiet, the sounds from the massive first floor sound system weren't as eminent at this altitude. Although, it did sound like some people were gathered in one of the back bedrooms. Rap music, that of DMX's *Party Up In Here* played from it. Which was normal. Brothers were always sliding off to do their own thing, especially in a house with 20 bedrooms, most of which were quite large with their own bathrooms; you never really knew what you'd find.

So, J.J. told them, "What's the difference, you ask?"

Tommy and Roberto looked at each other, and both shrugged their shoulders in their own ways.

"What is it?" Roberto said.

Tommy asked, "How does yours fit in?"

J.J. said, "It's simple. The Kappas are to other Latino frats what underground hip-hop is to commercial rap."

"What do you mean?" Roberto said.

"What I mean is," J.J. said, "it's like, this is where it's at. Where it's real. Where it originated, *whatever*. This ain't no Puffy shit. This is where it's raw. Because, fellas, this right here? This, is the truth."

Tommy said, "Well, if you're the truth… tell us if this is the truth."

J.J. was open to answering his question.

Tommy said, "We heard this house used to be a funeral parlor."

J.J. gave him a smirk. And said, "Tommy, I don't know nothing about that. But, what I do know? What I do know, is that this right here? The Valence University Chapter of The Kappa Latino Fraternity? This is more than just a frat. This, *is a Family*."

"J.J.!" Manveed said, happily, walking out of the back room where the people were hanging out. He was in a sweaty undershirt, still had the turban on his head and with his Kappa jersey flung over his shoulder shut the door behind him, walking in their direction, and asked: "How's the party?"

J.J. smiled. "You tell *me*."

Manveed inhaled, and said, upon exhale: "*Muchacho*."

He gave J.J. a fist bump and bounced down the stairs.

J.J. turned back to the freshmen: "What was I saying?"

"You were saying," Tommy said, "how it's a family here. But, you know, a lot of crews call themselves families. But, then, in the end? They all rat each other out."

"Word," Roberto said. "My experience, anyway."

"Well, look," J.J. said. "I can't speak on nobody else's experience. And I can't speak on no other crews. And I'm from The South Bronx, from the worst part, so believe me, I seen a lot. But, all I know, is that this right here? Right here, it's like living in a house with a bunch of different siblings. Because, we might not always get along. Shit, sometimes I wanna shoot some of these niggas my damn self. But, at the end of the day? No matter what? Any time any of us has ever needed a hand up? We have been there for each other, through thick and thin. Because, this right here, The Kappa House? It don't matter what the situation is. If there's a situation, without a doubt—we help each other out."

Roberto thought that was interesting.

But, he was no fool. He said: "Okay. But, can you give an example though?"

J.J. smiled. "Follow me."

With an air of confidence, he walked them across to the other side of the floor, to the room that Manveed had walked out of, put his hand on the knob, and said: "You asked for it."

J.J. shouted: "Diego!"

And opened the door.

To reveal: Little Diego in a dark blue, velvet bathrobe that said KAPPA on the back *slamming* the fat white chick from behind like a jackhammer as she gave Mario, sitting on a couch with sunglasses on like Ray Charles, his foot elevated and resting on a stool with ice on it… In short, her face went up and down on his giant log like she was washing it.

Diego turned to his Line Brother and said, "Hey, J.J., you got to get in on this shit right here, Bro! El Metro, baby!"

It was Kappa for *The Train.*

Diego slapped hands with Mario as they tag teamed her and said, "Brother bonding, meng!"

Mario moaned, "*Táto.*"

"Ray Charles!"

J.J. smiled, and looked at the freshmen: "Brotherhood, kid."

The last thing Hidalgo was thinking about. The last thing Hidalgo ever thought about. He pledged The Kappa looking for a Brotherhood. He pledged The Kappa while going through a dark time, and looking for support to help get through it. Instead, however, what he found was a group of Brothers that he *hated.*

As the party raged downstairs, Hidalgo, the senior, the creepy, Cuban homosexual in a silent war with a house full of machismo spread chalk into a large circle in his dark, candlelit room on the 3rd floor.

Inside of it, in the chalk, he drew a pentagram.

Hidalgo, a big guy, with narrow eyes, was wearing all white, proudly representing his roots in his native Santeria. This year, however, things would be different. This year, he would finally accomplish his goal of burning this Chapter to the ground.

And he would receive the proper help to properly do it.

On his knees within the pentagram, he lit the candles that he had spread around it.

Then, he began his quest into The Dark Arts—

The Black Magic—

He bowed his head, and asked for guidance…

He said: "Spirits of the house… *Dígame*."

THE CHAPTER

A Novel

Coming Soon
From Don Kasparoza

www.TheChapter.tv

Facebook.com/TheChapterTV

Twitter.com/TheChapterTV

ABOUT/FROM THE AUTHOR

Don Kasparoza grew up in Queens, New York. He graduated from Binghamton University, where he became a member of Phi Iota Alpha. His first novel, *For Blood And Loyalty*, was published in 2013. Feel free to connect with him at:

www.DonKasparoza.com

Facebook.com/DonKasparoza

Twitter.com/DonKasparoza

Instagram.com/DonKasparoza

And, if you liked this story, please:

Tweet it, Share it, and leave an honest review on Amazon, Goodreads, and any other place that will have you. It really does help a lot.

PS—While this may only be a short story, there are several people I would still very much like to Thank:

Ricardo Quiroz, La Pared, and The Brothers of Phi Iota Alpha Fraternity, Inc.

Thank you for your support.
–Don Kasparoza

FOR BLOOD AND LOYALTY

It's 1999, Bobby Drakis is 26, and after 6 very long years inside state prison he's out on appeal and finally back home in Bayside, Queens, New York City—where his best friend Victor Saravano has become a wealthy and dangerous drug dealing loan shark and enforcer for the mob. Hoping to avoid another 25-year sentence though, Bobby declines his offer for "a job" instead of getting paid like the rest of their childhood friends in Victor's crew are doing. But when an old flame brings him to his knees, and a chance encounter draws him into the life, shit hits the fan with force as true characters are revealed and dark secrets are brought to the surface as the people in their world fully realize that while blood might make you related…

It's Loyalty that makes you Family.

FOR BLOOD AND LOYALTY

A Novel about Love, Honor, and Fatherless Sons

By Don Kasparoza

Available on Amazon in Paperback and eBook

www.ForBloodAndLoyalty.com

Facebook.com/ForBloodAndLoyalty